The Frog Princess

For Alan

Kids Can Press acknowledges the financial support of the Ontario Arts Council,
the Canada Council for the Arts and the Government of Canada,
through the BPIDP, for our publishing activity.

Published in Canada by   Published in the U.S. by
Kids Can Press Ltd.   Kids Can Press Ltd.
29 Birch Avenue   2250 Military Road
Toronto, ON M4V 1E2   Tonawanda, NY 14150

www.kidscanpress.com

The artwork in this book was rendered in watercolor.
The text is set in Caslon 224 Book.

Edited by Debbie Rogosin
Designed by Julia Naimska
Printed and bound in Hong Kong, China, by Book Art Inc., Toronto

The hardcover edition of this book is smyth sewn casebound.
The paperback edition of this book is limp sewn with a drawn-on cover.

CM 01 0 9 8 7 6 5 4 3 2 1
CM PA 03 0 9 8 7 6 5 4 3 2 1

National Library of Canada Cataloguing in Publication Data

Allchin, Rosalind
The frog princess

ISBN 1-55337-000-7 (bound).   ISBN 1-55337-526-2 (pbk.)

I. Title.

PS8551.L5524F76 2001   jC813'.6   C2001-930174-X
PZ7.A44Fr 2001

Kids Can Press is a Corus™ Entertainment company

The Frog Princess

Written and illustrated by
Rosalind Allchin

Kids Can Press

Up at the palace the Royal Family was enjoying a hearty breakfast. The Prince ate quickly and hurried away. He had just enough time for a round of golf before the day's official duties began.

Down on the palace pond, Frog had forgotten about catching her breakfast. She was lost in her favorite daydream.

Suddenly her dream was interrupted by a loud splash.
"Oh, fiddlesticks," a voice grumbled. "Just when I was
doing so well. I'd give *anything* to find that wretched ball."

Frog looked up, and her eyes widened when she saw the Prince. Could daydreams really come true?

Silently she slipped into the water. She knew exactly where the ball had gone.

Frog leapt back onto the bank, clutching the ball. She quivered with excitement as she approached the Prince. He had promised *anything* as a reward for the ball, but there was only one thing she wanted.

"This ball for your hand in marriage," she croaked, and she puckered up her lips for a kiss.

The Prince stepped back in horror. However was he going to get out of this? A prince could never break his word, but the thought of marrying a frog made him shudder.

"You know, not everyone likes being a princess," he replied slowly. "Why not try it for a day and leave the kiss until midnight?"

Frog smiled and agreed. She could wait until midnight.

Frog hoped they would start their day with breakfast. But as soon as they arrived at the palace, she was whisked away to the Royal Wardrobe. She was squashed and squeezed into petticoats, dresses, shoes and wigs. Nothing seemed to fit. Changing into a princess was much more difficult than changing into a frog had been.

But when she was finally dressed, Frog could have danced for joy. She looked like a real princess! She wanted to stop and admire herself, but the Prince was in a hurry. He looked nervously at his watch and bustled her away to join the Royal Family on the balcony.

"Ready. Steady. Go!" the King commanded. And the
King, the Queen, the Prince, his grandmother, his sisters
and his cousins all began to smile and wave.

Down in the courtyard the crowd cheered and waved
back. Frog, beside herself with excitement, outsmiled and
outwaved them all.

The sun shone down. In her layers of silk and satin, Frog grew hotter and hotter. Her head drooped and far below something sparkling caught her eye. Without a thought she leapt over the parapet …

... into the cool waters of the palace moat.

When she came up for air, the Prince's pink face was looming above her.

"Coming in to join me?" she asked. "It's so lovely and cool."

But the Prince was not smiling.

"Princesses never get their clothes wet," he said.

Squeezed into another fabulous dress, Frog followed the Prince to the front door where the Royal Carriage was waiting.

She looked up and saw it had suddenly started to rain. Frog chuckled to herself. She wasn't going to make the same mistake again. Darting behind a pillar, she wriggled out of her clothes and dashed outside.

The Prince's face was an even deeper pink as he hustled Frog back inside.

"Princesses," he hissed, "never take their clothes off in public."

Frog hung her head and prepared to struggle back into the dress.

"Did you say we were lunching on a ship?" Frog asked hopefully when they were seated in the carriage at last.

But the Prince shook his head wearily. "We're launching a ship, not lunching," he said.

So Frog was surprised and pleased when she was presented with an enormous bottle of champagne. "What fun," she thought as she popped the cork and took a long drink. The bubbles tickled her nose. She burped and giggled and forgot for a moment how hungry she was.

But once again the Prince was not pleased. "You were supposed to throw the bottle at the ship, not drink from it," he sighed. "Now we're going to award the prizes at a tournament. Please try to act like a proper princess."

20

The jousting was very exciting, but Frog didn't enjoy it at all. She was too worried about how she should behave. Life as a princess was so confusing.

A waiter handed her a glass. The woman next to her was sipping her drink, but Frog had learned that lesson. She looked around. The Prince was lifting his glass and nodding toward the victorious knight. Frog smiled in relief. She raised her arm high and sent her glass sailing through the air.

The Prince took Frog firmly by the arm and marched her away.

"I think we'll take a break from our official duties and go fishing," he said grimly.

Frog sat on the bank of the Royal Pond and watched as the Prince opened a box and selected a delicious worm. She licked her lips — lunch at last! But to her dismay, the Prince threaded the worm on a hook, closed the box and lowered the hook into the water.

They sat for a very long time. Nothing happened. Nothing at all.

Frog was bored. Being a princess wasn't as much fun as she'd expected, and she was so hungry. Didn't princesses ever eat? The Prince looked so cross she didn't dare ask.

She brightened up when the Prince looked at his watch and said it was time for tea with the Queen.

Frog wished that just once a princess could do something without first changing her dress, but the promise of food kept her going.

In the Queen's parlor she was handed a steaming cup of tea and a plate piled with cakes and sandwiches. Her mouth watered and her stomach gurgled — but the food stayed on her plate.

The Prince had warned her that princesses never eat and talk at the same time, and the Queen kept asking her questions.

"How many children would you like to have?" she asked just as Frog was about to take a bite.

"Two or three hundred will do for a start," sighed Frog, and to her surprise everyone laughed. She talked her way right through teatime without swallowing a single crumb.

The day was to end with a grand ball. This was what Frog had dreamed about, but as she climbed the stairs for yet another change of clothes, a tear trickled down her cheek. So far, life as a princess hadn't been at all what she'd expected. And although she was trying so hard to please, she never seemed to get anything right.

She cheered up when she entered her room. A maid had run a bath for her and she couldn't wait to get in. A plunge in the water would feel like home.

But … Frog stopped, poised on the edge of the tub. She remembered the rules about princesses not taking their clothes off and not getting them wet. Whatever would a princess do now? The more she thought about it, the more uncertain she became.

When the Prince tapped on her door, she was still sitting by the bath trying to puzzle it out. In a panic she pulled on her ballgown over her tea dress and hurried out.

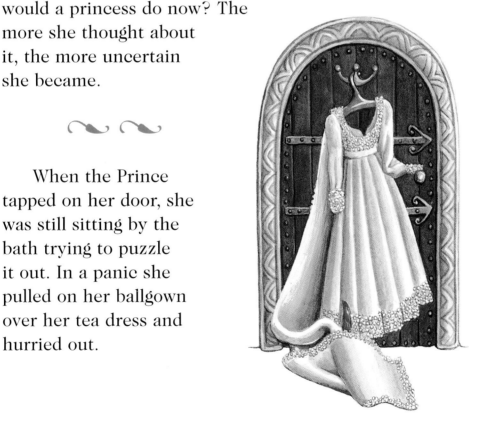

The ballroom was packed with people all eager to meet Frog. But Frog was too hungry even to think about doing her royal duty. Among the crowd she spotted servants bearing trays of food. She steered the Prince toward the largest tray.

Her eyes grew round with horror at what she saw
heaped on the platter before her.

And as she stared, the clock began to strike midnight.

As the last chime faded away, the Prince turned
reluctantly toward Frog. It was time for the promised kiss.
    But all he saw were fluttering curtains at an open window,
an abandoned shoe and an overturned tray of frogs legs.
    And through the window drifted the words …

I am not a princess …..
I am a ….. frooooooooooooog

followed by the faintest splash.